EQUATING THE EQUATIONS OF INSANITY

EQUATING THE EQUATIONS OF INSANITY

A Journey from Grief to Victory

DURGESH SATPATHY

PARTRIDGE
A Penguin Random House Company

ISBN:	Softcover	978-1-4828-4701-7
	eBook	978-1-4828-4700-0

Print information available on the last page.

To order additional copies of this book, contact
Partridge India
000 800 10062 62
orders.india@partridgepublishing.com

www.partridgepublishing.com/india

Contents

To my daughter, Aashi,
Every time I look into her eyes, I get a
positive inspiration to serve humanity.
Bless You.

To the readers,

When I ride my bike, I do ride it at an average speed of 80 KMPH, when my wife is with me it's about 60 KMPH, and when my Mum is in the back seat it reduces to 50 KMPH. Neither my Mum nor my wife say to do so but inside my mind some equation runs and I get the required speed.

For every situation in life, our mind equates some equations, and trust me this book is all about equations of human life, by equating them anyone can get rid of grief in any form and be able to develop a new way of life.

Everyday unavoidable bad news we perceive... Accidents are daily incidents... Nature is filled with such horrors that shock our mind all times... We experience death and agony with growing age...

All of these experiences left us with a negative mental state and we waste our positivity...

A misdeed or crime implies punishment to criminals in human society. What about the sufferers then? Sufferers are left with a mental state and nothing cures their introvert mind. This book attempts to cure it.

This book will retrieve your positivity amidst any living condition.

Like Nature equates all delicacies of life, this book answers your inner equations.

Acknowledgements

I am indebted to my parents for their blessings for all my dreams and aspirations. Their constant support throughout my life has made me what I am now. I extend my deep sense of thankfulness to my wife Dr. Pratichee Panigrahi for her continuous trust in me and my work.

I express special thanks:

To Mr. Haresh Satpathy, Research Scholar, P.G. Department of English, Sambalpur University for editing and proof-reading this work. Without his support I couldn't have succeeded in this endeavor.

To Mr. Abhijit Mishra, student of B. Tech, VSSUT Burla for his contribution in sketch works for this book.

To Partridge Publishing and it's team especially Mr. Joe Anderson and Jeric Romano for their guidance.

To Praneet, Barun, Abhiti, my other colleagues for their praiseworthy suggestions and feedbacks.

Chasing the Unknown

"Did you really want to die?
No one commits suicide because
they want to die.
Then why do they do it? Because
they want to stop the pain."
-Tiffanie DeBartalo

Sitting beneath an endless sky; unknown corner somewhere on earth, "She is solitary, someone kept her in dark." She locked the door and lost the key. Her life has gone insane screaming in agony, solitude & pain. Tear left a trial upon her delicate skin as she used to cry for whole days. Growing up, she never thought she will be at this place. The saddest part is that she has to work, shielding her suffering inside. She is paralyzed with her lateral thoughts, doing nothing except crying & crying.

"Every incident in this earth is either an accident colliding with our peaceful life, or our creation to gain a better life."

God is maintaining his distance, or he is not there. If God subsists, he must be a good being, doting, caring, puissant and eliminates frivolous pain inside us. Our noetic conceptions, our feelings, our goals, our memories are our own creation and there is no role of God in it. Neither angels nor demons, neither the present nor the future, neither height nor depth, neither death nor life; nothing is portrayed by God.

"God is a creation of human brain."

There must be no other things other than God; people spend most of their time to search for. There is no religion in this world that can portray the real image of God. It's a belief that he looks like a human being as we thought so. The contractors of God preach that "he creates, he acts, he loves and he commands." Further he develops bonding in relationship upon meditation and prayers. Shall we need to ask God every time we suffer? Is suffering, a component of our life? Why God has only culled innocent hearts and not the criminals?

Passion makes us stop eating and sleeping, just we sense the peace for it. They are architects of our thoughts, but for her it was different. She is isolated inside the four walls of a dark room. She is not able to sleep with such painful memories, she used to wake up at midnights or early hours in the morning;

suffering throughout the day from her eye strain. She lost her appetite and experienced changes in her weight. Simple task becomes difficult and takes longer time to complete; she is just physically drained.

"Some wounds; never reflects on the skin, but kills us slowly from inside."

She started feeling agitated; sometimes even violent and short tempered. She started experiencing physical complaints like headache, back pain and stomach pain. She started harming herself by biting her body. She started smoking & consuming alcohol. She is not aware why she is harming herself but it seems to her as if she is trying to kill the pain inside. Searching for something but getting nothing, not a single hint.

"She never wished for the thing what she is experiencing. It is her inner voice that became her enemy."

It seems like the sun stopped shining for her. Defeated in the race of staying alive; she asks herself "what is the purpose of her life? Why she is alive?" Her inner voice always knocked her heart to say, "You are not needed by anyone anymore, you are useless." She has no other option than hurting herself.

Shocked with emotional pain her inner voice is saying, "You have no solutions for your wounds; you can't share your pains." It's difficult to convey her grief to anyone when she doesn't have faith in herself. She is confused if she needs solution to her problem or to compromise with the death patriarchs.

She is not able to control her negative thoughts no matter how much she tried. Acting like she is searching for a hint that can help her to get closer to her "last wish." She started calling her dear ones to say "don't care for me anymore; everything will get its glow after me."

"She disappeared; her voice, her laughter and the warmth of her breath never seen by no one again."

A sunny day in the month of June, 2013; it is one of the saddest days of her life when she wished to QUIT. Kelly, her daughter is 11 years old, born & brought up in a crucial life situation; she is self-critical and always required positive feedback for life. That day Kelly went to Sugar Land Prep, a residential school at Houston, she had to join the boarding school just because her father wanted to. Hiding her tears inside, she dropped Kelly at the school and returned home. As usual her husband went for his office and nobody knows what happened next.

That day evening when Jenifer's husband returned home he found her suicide note.

> Dear Kelly,
>
> I don't find a reason to wake up and get out of bed, not for a cup of coffee or your sweet kiss, no work to do, no train

to catch, no one to hold my hand. My Mum always said "not to be sensitive and to develop thick skins around, just to avoid being hurt" and I always used to reply "by this nobody can make me happy too."

This world may accept me but I can't face it, so I am doing what seems to be the best thing for me. I am not broken I am not cheated neither misused by my loved ones. I am sorry that I am a looser and could not fix the things on my way. I am tired and can't face this terrible period of life.

I stopped trusting people neither God. Mum used to say "God has an eye at everything and punish us after our death for our sins"; I want to meet that super hero named God; if he really exists.

I love you Mum.

I love you Dad.

I love you Anni, my cute sister.

Goodbye Kelly.

With love
Jenifer

"People say that she is alive but nobody knows where she is?"

A Zoo for a Unicorn

Jenifer is born on 23rd day in the month of June 1975. Since her birth she wants to give some message to this world, she was little hurry to come to this world; she came almost four weeks early. Her Mum was so scared about her health, but finally everything went well followed by proper post delivery care. The new born baby was very cute and attractive, with an infectious smile.

It's hard to remember things of infancy period, and she has never heard about it from her parents too; but some memories of her recent past were still captured in her sub conscious mind as she had heard many times from her grandma. Since early infancy stage she was awesome like a sweet Barbie doll, cried little, smiled more and slept very well.

She started talking when she was nine months only and with times she developed herself very talkative.

"Being in home is like magic moments, in a magic world, among magicians."

At early childhood she was the center of attraction among all kids in her family. For her parents she was like a little magician, who has the power to make anyone happy. She became a good companion of her father; she used to go to the Church along with him sitting on his shoulder having a feeling like a queen.

In those days church was a nice destination for family gatherings, especially at Christmas times. Everyone instructed her to dress in a different way, sometimes she got warnings like "if she doesn't dress like a queen they will leave her at home," but she followed her guts and wore an outfit like a groom.

During Christmas they spent around one to two hours at Church and its partying time for her; she walked here and there inside. Her Mum wished "no one should know that Jenifer is with her." However the people around there even the preachers; picked Jenifer and played with her.

She had a strong faith on Santa Claus and his mysterious planet where kids have a chance to fulfill their secret desires; she believed that those myths are more than stories to delight children; she always expected gifts and cakes from Santa. This beautiful culture of her family made her feel as the luckiest kid of her big family.

She missed those days not just because she had good neighbors, and some sweet friends to play with, but because she was a part of a family with high traditional values where every member has respect for each other.

For his dad she was his best buddy, but she finds her Mum as her best friend still she was in Kindergarten. During the early days at kindergarten she used to cry and wanted her Mum to be with her all the time as she has to stay with strangers all day; till the time she was not acquainted with other kids.

Every day her mother has to walk about three kilometers, to drop Jenifer at kindergarten, early in the morning at around 6.00am, and pick her back on afternoon around 2.00 PM. On insistence of Jenifer in early days her Mum has to spend some times in kindergarten, in spite of her teacher's displeasure. Today everything is like some memories of her dreams "of a magic world" and it disappears always once she wakes up.

"Everything looks beautiful in books and not in real life, my childhood is like a golden dream for me and I am missing those days." -Jenifer

She was into a joint family, a large family of baby boomers; she was 5th of eighteen children and she was the most lovable kid among those eighteen. Her parents had 3 children along with her brother Steve and her sister Anni. Anni and Jenifer were twins and Steve was the youngest in her family.

Her father has two brothers and four sisters. And this number was just an average during that time. Both of her uncle's were into farming; that is a seasonal source of income, so day to day expenses of the family had to be taken care of by his father and partially supported by the female members of the family.

Helen, Jenifer's Mum was working part time in a boutique, she was busy and equally responsible to sustain the family. Jake, her father was working as a taxi driver. For the outside world Jake is an honest, worm and helpful person, but he has a different face from inside.

Her grandma was conservative in nature while his grandfather was one of the coolest men of her life.

Anni and Jenifer both loved to hear stories from her grandfather and asked them lots of silly questions. When her grandfather got tired, he has number of tricks to engage them and the most common one is asking some puzzles. He was working in a farm, where Jenifer and Anni used to play with chickens, the chickens were her favorite and they used to help feed them.

They fed them their food and the most disgusting thing was they fed them with "dead insects." Once they find baby chickens; they were taking them home to play with.

Her glossy life didn't last for long, after the birth of Steve her parents started disliking her and Anni, as her grandparents were of conservative thoughts and "being a girl child is a curse for the family" in that society where they used to stay.

She has witnessed a number of ups and downs in her life, acts of domestic violence "on her Mum by her father." When things became very critical, and it started affecting life of Jenifer, on request of Helen, Jenifer started staying at Sherin's (Helen's brother) place.

"I have never seen such a child who is so broken physically and emotionally." -Sherin

For Jenifer, her Uncle's place is a perfect home to live in. Her aunt Shibi likes discipline and cleanliness; she always wants not any dust particle may be located on any shelf or corner inside the room. Not only Shibi ensures that her own home is clean, but she also takes good care that everyone else should also stay in a perfectly organized manner with place for everything and everything in place. Even when she used to visit Jenifer's place she cleans her room and makes things organized.

Her uncle and aunt wanted her to forget what she had experienced, when she was with her parents, but her nightmares showed a different story. She was not able to forget her sad and fearful past. Her uncle and aunt realized that things were beyond their control, it's not in their ability to regenerate that happiest mood of Jenifer again. Even after lots of efforts made, they were not able to recreate the psychological blocks of the crushed soul.

Then they are forced to consult with a Child therapist, who suggested keeping her away from negative thoughts, movies and such life events that may remind her painful past. After four weeks, her uncle and aunt realized that she is recovering when she started playing normally with other children and stopped playing scenes of violence and death.

"God gifted a Zoo; with a paralyzed care taker."

Those who have faith in God please pray for her dad. When Shibi got a call from Helen, she replied "he met with an accident, pray for him, God is taking care of him that is why he is alive." But for Jenifer "God is just an imagination, a creation of human brain" if he is there, he must be enjoying like an audience of her real life show.

The scene behind was "John, Jenifer's dad met with an accident while coming back from work late night." People say a lady lost control of her car and hit him; he was bleeding in his head and the lady left immediately.

There was no taxi nearby, and it takes too long by the ambulance to reach there, bleeding was quite critical, and as an outcome of it he is now paralyzed. He had a surgery, but that didn't work.

Finally complete burden of her family was under the responsibility of her Mum. After a few years when Jenifer became10 years old her aunt gave birth to a baby boy. Shibi started devoting much of her times to the new born baby and Jenifer started feeling neglected. Jenifer developed a feeling that her Mum needs some more support to take care of his father. So she finally came back home again.

The Orgasmic Psychological Experiments

Even though Jenifer knows that tomorrow is merely a promissory note; still she has some hope left in her heart, for a better future of her Mum and Anni. Every time she looks to her Mum's face she thanks God for making her strong enough to face this crucial part of her life. She does extend all possible support as per her strengths; even though she is a small kid of 10 years old.

The little heart manages to survive with all these pains and now she is determined to give her best. She got good grades in school, she performs well at sports, and she manages things at home perfectly. But there is something in her mind that is not allowing her to forget her painful past.

To the outside world, "she is confident, pretty and smart" but everything is artificial. After a couple of years her paralyzed father didn't able to speak, and he didn't survive for long and died after two months. After this tragedy, along with her Mum they struggled a lot, to go on with their lives. She is unable to ignore that pain until a day when she meets Harry, Helen's ex-boyfriend.

"Someone carries my belief that raises hope in me, but flame didn't last for long." -Jenifer

Jenifer is only twelve years of age when Harry shifts to her place. With the presence of Harry, Jenifer finds a positive change in her Mum's life. It is a great pleasure for Jenifer that, after a long dark past, her Mum is enjoying some happy moments, what Jenifer wanted to built from years, was built in a day. Within a short span of time Harry manages to win the heart of Jenifer too.

Harry pretends to be very nice and always offers her gifts and chocolates.

Harry was working in a power plant, and after few months he started working on night shift. During those days when he finds Jenifer alone at home, he started doing things that made her scared, he used to rub her legs and tell her "you have a nice pair of legs, you are so cute, and I always wanted to be with you." Being a teenager, she was not much aware of sex, even like "she couldn't get pregnant by kissing or touching private parts." The other reason why she was scared is "the person who was doing all this stuff was her Mum's boyfriend."

He used to touch her in a weird way and wanted to do all dirty stuff. She tried to avoid him, but she was not able to do so.

"Tell me what good touch is and what is bad for I am young and I have no dad."

She was confused how to tell her Mum about such dirty acts of Harry and how she will react after knowing this. She was not able to share among her friends too because she felt like they may look down on her. Once when she was feeling very upset and sitting at a corner of her room, Helen tried to get some inputs from her. Jenifer replied "I hate him the way he behaves, he is not a good guy" Helen got angry and slapped her; without knowing the fact.

Jenifer tried to tell her the truth "how he behaves with her when Helen is not around, he touches her in a scary way." Helen didn't convince with her and said "stop creating a scene between us, it might be a coincidence." Helen further suggested "you should avoid wearing short dresses at home." Her words hurt Jenifer deeply from inside as she thought "In Helen's view it's my fault." When situation became too worse, Jenifer decided to spend most of her times with friends. She didn't able to express her grief with anyone and felt crushed from inside always.

When her friends asked about her mood, she responded, "I hate my new dad, he is not a good guy"; but feel embarrassed inside to say the truth. It created a gap between Jenifer and her Mum. Helen usually advices Jenifer to be at home but she denies because she was not happy with the things going around. She started to develop negative feelings for her Mum, and she didn't bother if her Mum really cares for her.

When Jenifer reached 10th grade, she was sent away to a girl's boarding school against her consent, but the good thing happened was a dozen of her childhood friends were there and it's a really nice school; known for its discipline and academic excellence. It is a private, religious school at Houston and her Mum paid a good amount to send her there.

Jenifer was keenly interested in theatre and music since childhood. She wanted to join a music class, so she opted for music as a part of the extra curriculum requirements. Miss Katty was her music teacher. Jenifer used to trust Katty and with times a bond has developed between both of them; because of Katty's kindness and caring nature. Jenifer finds a reflection of her Mum's image in Katty. She started sharing all her pains to Katty, and she gets some relief out of it. Initially it was very awkward and complicated to share such unusual things, but with certain times she started revealing all secrets of her life.

"Nothing is permanent in my mysterious world, even my moments of belief," -Jenifer

After six months Katty offered Jenifer to share her room and Jenifer agreed instantly; in search of love and care from her. Katty didn't able to hide her real face for long, within few days Jenifer got to know the ugly character of Katty; she started to take undue advantages of her helplessness and continued the horrible model that her life had claimed.

Jenifer was at the hands of a person who is admired by her students and society for her position, but things were horrific for Jenifer. At night Katty came to her bed and started playing the dirty game; leaving her wrecked than she had ever been. She used to show her pornographic clips and started doing malicious acts with her. Further played with her private parts with fingers; it hurts a lot to Jenifer, but she was helpless.

Most of the time Jenifer was with her, she did not have clothes on her and sometimes she made her dress up in lingerie; her respects turns into horror by the time.

She recollects all her energy and wish to move out from these four walls of debility and fight against this act of brutality. She started searching all such students who are suffering from this pain and someone like Katty is taking undue advantages of them. She finds a dozen of such cases in her class and for all those cases the demon was Katty.

She energizes courage of all those girls and motivates them to put their story in front of Management. Finally management convinces with the fact and terminates Katty.

Flipped a Coin for a Cake

He is tall, handsome, and kind hearted, a shy guy; known for his rough life model, joins the college. He doesn't bother what is going on inside the campus. A collection of music from Nirvana and a pair of earphone plugged in his ears is the fuel for his life. Most of the time he can be seen in a Grunge outfit and holding a Guitar in his hands. His best social tool was that "he was a songwriter and Guitarist."

It might be the thought of the outside world; but from inside David imagines a different kind of life for him. He always asked himself some scary questions "why he is living? What is the purpose of his living?" He wanted to gather huge success in his life; but how he didn't know.

He wanted to be a successful automobile engineer or a Guitarist; actually he was confused of his goal. God might have scripted something else for him. Miss Lily was his physics teacher; the sexiest lady in the campus, for him a sex bomb. Every guy in the campus wanted to have her in his dream; David too. Mr. Mario was his music teacher; a tall and rude gentleman having a broad face with a countable hairs in the head.

"It was a new chapter in the life of Jenifer, a new flavor she was waiting for."

The first day "I'm telling you - the guy was a complete stranger, just walked up and picked my bag and dropped it at music class and he disappeared," - Jenifer said to Anni

Anni: "You're too good for this world; everybody loves to help you."

Jenifer: "For some reason, I got attracted to him. He is so dashing and cute dear!"

Anni: "How, exactly, do you think that for an unknown?"

Jenifer: "I was just checking you out; I was just kidding."

This is the way how Jenifer met David; the cool David's way. In the music classes they became friends. It was a perfect match "as David was a lyricist and Jenifer was a fan of music and theatre; both of them were a fan of Kurt Cobain with a passion for Psychedelic Rock music."

David's Mum was worried that, David was a shy guy and quiet in nature, sometimes he doesn't behave well with girls. She has already discussed with his father several times, but did not find any solution out of it.

One day David's Mum asked him "Give me one good reason why I should wear a hot dress."

David smiled and didn't respond.

Mum: "You were always the quiet one; you did not speak to girls well. Sometimes I am scared of you. Are you happy with your life or searching something beyond my expectations?"

David: "I am getting your point and nothing as such issue with me I am a perfect man, not a gay. I have someone in my life."

Her Mum felt relaxed with his inputs and thanked God that everything is normal.

In a sunny day David was sitting inside the classroom, he was confused with his thoughts; he slept for a while and dreamt of an angel. He walked into another world, where he found himself surrounded by some golden clouds and a dazzling sphere of atmosphere. He was sitting in a golden chair; some beautiful girls were serving him wine, a beautiful angel with blue eyes and hot legs came near him and said "David, from years, whom I was searching for is none other than you, you are the love of my life and she hugged him" A sparkling ray came from her eyes and a stormy sound occurred from the silence. David started shouting, help, help, then opened his eyes.

He found himself in the arms of Jenifer. Jenifer slapped him and said "stupid come out of your dreams." David smiled from inside and left the room, his expressions has the power to create a question in the mind of Jenifer. Was it love?

After a few days they started a rock band "Zeolite"; with Jenifer as the lead singer. After a couple of months; they received a letter to participate in a rock concert and it was their first assignment. Jenifer in a hurry filled the form, but she was confused too, whether to participate or not, as till date they have not performed in such a big event. Finally it ends up with a positive move.

They participated, and the show was quite good; they came third in the concert. To start with it was satisfactory.

They celebrated for the day, gone for a movie, they made love (David was the first guy, Jenifer slept with, seemed incidental or anecdotal but true), but she was not aware that it would cost her to an unforgettable pain in future. After few days they had to leave the college on completion of course. Jenifer approached him for living together at her place, but David asked for some more time (he wanted to consult with his family). Jenifer was not able to read the mind of David. Every morning at 9 AM he used to call Jenifer and told her "attendance for the day"; followed by a promise of Jenifer to call her everyday whenever he may be.

Jenifer was appointed as music teacher in a school at Houston; a career she always wished for. She faced days with joys and sorrows of solitude at job. With times David started avoiding Jenifer, he pretended to be busy all the time. A day came when David explained why they could not go with the old relationship (it was obvious for Jenifer, the same old story; David's family would never agree for a girl with such family background). Jenifer was putting a lot of pressures but none of her effort worked.

One day she got a call from David and he said "I don't want to receive any call from you, please stop trying to contact me again;" it was all over.

In a winter morning she was on leave, the day was Dec 24th 1995; coincidentally, it was David's birthday she ordered a birthday cake online for David. She instructed to write over the cake "I am sorry, with a smiley" and requested not to disclose her name. When the courier boy reached David's place David refused to receive the same without knowing the name of the sender. Finally she has to instruct the guy to disclose her name, and as expected David did not receive the cake. Jenifer called him almost 50 times that day to wish him but he did not respond to her call. She cried throughout the day. She called David's friend Imran to convey that "she wanted to wish him." Finally at 11.48PM he picked her call and Jenifer said "Thanks for everything" and David cut the phone.

"Love never hurts, cheating hurts."

Life became very critical for Jenifer. Jenifer was so blind in love that she didn't find a reason to live. On a weekend she was going for her aunt Shibi's place. She found Imran (David's friend) at a cafeteria. Imran tried to justify the reasons of David's behavior; Imran revealed all untold stories of David's past. Before David met Jenifer he was in a relationship with Ihana, bonding between them was very strong and it lasted almost four years.

Due to some unavoidable reasons they got separated but now everything is probably ok.

Ihana, a Software engineer, was well settled at Boston and belongs to a rich family. David's father and Ihana's uncle are childhood friends. David's parents have already accepted Ihana as their "daughter in law" but there was some issue with Ihana's family that might be the reasons behind their separation, but everything is ok now as David is well settled. Imran explained "what was David's look from outside was not the actual reflection of what he was from inside".

After few days Jenifer got the information of David's Engagement. Even though David got engaged he wanted to have relationship with Jenifer. As Jenifer was staying alone in a flat at Huston, David started taking undue advantages of her. He used to come to her place and had physical relationship with Jenifer. Jenifer was so blind in love that she was not able to justify herself what was right and what was wrong. After six months of David's engagement he got married to Ihana, and he settled with Ihana.

Jenifer flipped a coin for a cake, and the cake was her life; she was not aware that both head and tail will go in favor of David. She decided not to marry throughout her life; justifying herself "I will not be able to love anyone in rest of my life"

When She Tried to Hug a Tiger

Jenifer met her husband at Boston; she was staying there for about six months while working for HOPE, an NGO working for women welfare, health and Safety. She was leading a workshop for awareness among women towards health & safety. Roach was a motivational coach who came there for a one week motivational program for the members of the HOPE. Roach with his team stayed there for about one week where they conducted one to one interaction with each members.

Jenifer was highly influenced by traits of Roach, and afterwards it became her weakness.

The friendship lasted for around one year before it has taken the shape of a marital relationship, she got married to Roach followed by a twelve months friendship. They planned for their honeymoon at Singapore after two weeks, but something different was written in her fate. Roach had to go for a three months program at London as Roach didn't want to miss the opportunity considering its value addition.

Roach's session went well, and he came back after three months and it was celebration time.

They went to a restaurant but coincidentally Paul, a friend of Roach joined them, during that one hour of conversation Jenifer shared her story "how she met Roach and the transition from friendship to marriage."

Roach: I don't want to talk to you.

Paul: Hey I am sorry, didn't able to join you people at your marriage.

Jenifer: Roach is right.

Paul: Are you taking his side against me?

Jenifer: Yeah…it's obvious he is my hubby.

Paul: umm… please, please, please don't be like kids.

Jenifer: It looks like you're in trouble. Can I help?

Paul: Please Jenifer.

Jenifer: Just commit you will pay the bill.

Paul is a chatter box, and how time was spent with him Jenifer didn't know.

Roach had to go for a meeting after an hour so he dropped Jenifer at home and went there. In the evening when he reached home, he was feeling upset he didn't talk with Jenifer for an hour, when Jenifer tried to get some inputs Roach said, "It's beyond my imagination, you were flirting with Paul." Jenifer was shocked for a moment and even though it was not her fault, she politely apologized for the same.

After her apology Roach cooled down and considered it was his fault and said sorry. Jenifer has experienced a change in the behavior of Roach afterwards, but she was surprised with the excessive care by him, but it was not love its inferiority. Jenifer started creating wings for her dreams, life went smoothly for one year and Roach has also proved himself a good husband. As a part of HOPE every member has to go for a psychological counseling course and it was a one year part time program.

Jenifer didn't want to join the course as she has to attend the classes on weekends, but Roach forced her to join the course, as it's free of cost and she will get benefited too in her career profile.

She joined the program and Roach started taking undue advantages of it; most of the weekends he can be seen with his friends parting and drinking at home. Things became critical when he started making relation with his ex-girlfriend again and it was brought to the notice of Jenifer. Upon the interference of Paul, Roach promised Jenifer "I will never meet her again, and never hurt you too." The scene settled down there.

Jenifer completed the psychological counseling program and things were gone well for a couple of months.

It was the day of their marriage anniversary; the tie completed three years, and they planned for a celebration. In the evening while celebrating for the day, Jenifer reported headache. In the next morning she consulted with her doctor and she suggested for pregnancy test and the result was positive. Roach congratulated her and promised that "he will take care of both of them and will never give a chance to regret."

Her faith didn't last for long, Roach punched her in the stomach and her condition became critical.

The scene was, "that day he reached home drunk, at late night and it was obvious for Jenifer to be angry as she was staying alone at home for the whole day, in spite of her last stage of pregnancy. Roach was not able to control himself and punched her." She got admitted in hospital, and she gave birth to a baby girl, Kelly. The baby was alright but both of them had to stay at ICU for next one week considering criticality of the case.

"Fate is not pre-written, we create our own." –Jenifer

Everything what she was experiencing is an outcome of the decision of her past, what is going on in her life was written by herself. She can't blame anybody as she has chosen her way with Roach. She was little scared with the behavior of Roach, she decided to move on. She left him and move away with her new born baby. She shifted to Riana's place, one of her colleague at HOPE. When Roach didn't find her at home, he tried to contact all her colleagues, to Riana as well. Riana acted like she is not aware where she is and convinced him to support him to find her.

With Riana and Kelly, Jenifer didn't feel the absence of Roach in her life. Kelly grew up to two years of age and Jenifer has almost forgotten her past and she has only one goal in her life, to give a better foundation to Kelly's life. Roach got to know that Jenifer is staying with Riana; he went there and started pleading in front of her, he said "I am no longer the old cruel Roach, after you left me I have changed a lot, please give me a last chance."

Riana also suggested Jenifer to give him another chance, considering the future of Kelly.

Jenifer strengthened her belief and come back with him. They had some good times together; she thought her love may mould him with time. Roach started representing himself in such a way that it met the emotional requirements of Jenifer. In the initial six months Roach acted in such a way that Jenifer started to change her mind and when she was about to convince, Roach politely requested her to quit the Job, to take care of Kelly, he further added if you feel to join your job in future, you can rejoin at any time.

For a mother her daughter's care is everything, she agreed with Roach and quit her job. Things were gone well for the next couple of months, and then he started showing her real face to Jenifer. Slowly he started playing with her self esteem, with his abusive words. Slowly she started realizing that she is useless; it took pace when he started threatening in the name of Kelly. She was in such grief and depression for almost two years and she didn't know when he started physical violence.

Finally she evidenced a time when it crossed the limits when she had to live away from Kelly; she was paralyzed for a moment and started writing the suicide note.

Lateral Equations of Insanity

"You are after all, what you think.
Your emotions are the slaves to your
thoughts, and you are the slave to your
emotions." -Elizabeth Gilbert

It really hurts when Kelly looks behind her life. Even though God has justified thousands of reasons to live, living a life without the love of parents is one of the darkest scenes as portrayed by the super power. She was not able to convince herself with the fact that her Mum is no more.

She was asking herself "If Jenifer is no more, why she didn't left a clue that she is dead?" To get the answer she started searching for all unsolved clues of Jenifer's life.

It's almost ten years after the suicide of Jenifer; Kelly met with William, an Industrialist from Texas. Later she was married to him. Within a short span of time William proved to be a true companion for her faint emotional life. Kelly conveyed him all saddest episodes of her life. Then they decided to go with a private detective agency to find if there is any clue left. For the first three months of initial investigation, they did not find any clue. Kelly was not happy with the outcomes of the detective agency and they wanted to stop the investigation.

In the same day Kelly and William has gone for a function at Shibi's place, where she found the personal diary of Jenifer. Kelly was shocked with some realities what she got inside.

"I have gone through various domestic
violence statistics of United Nations
Study and it shocked me from inside
knowing the facts. It's not only me
there are millions of people who are
suffering from cruel acts by their
partners or their family members
or by society." -Jenifer

On an average, 24 people per minute are victims of rape, physical violence or stalking by an intimate partner in the United States.

(Source:http://www.cdc.gov/violenceprevention/pdf/ipv_factsheet2012-a.pdf)

One in four women (24.3%) and 1 in 7 men (13.8%) aged 18 and older in the United States have been the victim of severe physical violence by an intimate partner in their lifetime.

(Source:http://www.cdc.gov/violenceprevention/intimatepartner violence/consequences.html)

From 1994 to 2010, about 4 in 5 victims of intimate partner violence were female.

(Source: http://www.bjs.gov/content/pub/pdf/ipv9310.pdf)

More than 1 in 3 women (35.6%) and more than 1 in 4 men (28.5%) in the United States have experienced rape, physical violence and/or stalking by an intimate partner in their lifetime.

(Source: http://www.cdc.gov/violenceprevention/pdf/nisvs_report2010-a.pdf)

Jenifer has experienced immense of lateral thoughts followed by loss and grief. Untold painful memories, thoughts of suicide, disbelief on God were forcing her to kill herself. She thought of the life of those millions of people like her who were the actors of some cruel stories which were written as a part of their fate. Some unknown force was telling her from inside: "before you die, you should know what actually forcing you to kill yourself." Somehow she manages to boost her morale and prepared herself to taste the lateral equations of Insanity. She started searching for people like her who have experienced pains in their life and not getting away to move on.

As per her diary she has met so many people suffering from loss and grief and she discovered:

"It's not grief it's the unsolved lateral equations of insanity that killing them."

Nine such abstracts from her diary are
mentioned here where grievers or their
near ones have been able to find out
the lateral equations of insanity.

Pilot of Darkness

> "If pain must come, may it come
> quickly, because I have a life to live,
> and I need to live it in the best way
> possible. If he has to make a choice,
> may he make it now. Then I will
> either wait for him or forget him."
> – Paulo Coelho

An innocent 25 years old lady, who comes from a poor family background, lives in a small house, tends to complain a lot. She was not always like this but situation forced her...

She was born in a joint family and was always proud of, for the love and care she got. She has experienced a trouble free life until she became sixteen, but at that point, life began to change. She started experiencing the real taste of this beautiful world, not the smell of earth but the true face of people around her.

The casual life of this young girl took a sharp turn as Clinton came into her life.

The young girl was actually stuck within a dream world, a world from which there was only one way out and this 'dream person' would show the way. Suspicious of this situation, but somewhat trusting of this person, the young girl oddly willingly agreed to the proposal, but for some reason a nagging feeling of 'this is a bad choice' won't go away but what if this boy couldn't be relied upon. Or what if everything told is completely true? How could an ordinary young girl be this important to the situation? No turning back now though.

When love is in heart,
the height of Everest
too looks small." -Katrina

Since childhood Katrina was a fan of Art and Theatre. She joins a theatre group at an age of 16. Within one month she got a chance to work as a child actor. Clinton was her costar in that play. She was quite nervous as it was her debut stage performance, it was Clinton's day; he boosted her morale, and she got attracted towards him. The show has gone well. When love is in the air everything looks beautiful, Katrina was enjoying the longest depth of love.

She started searching clues that,"if heat is on the other side too" and she succeeded when he asked her for a date after a week.

Katrina turned nineteen, and they started planning for their marriage. Till that time she was driving her life journey alone, now it's Clinton's turn to sit on the driver's seat. The road was smooth, but he didn't want to travel through the safest way. And he proved it after marriage, within a short span of time. Things became critical when arguments turned into an act of domestic violence. She never revealed her worst days to anyone, with a hope in mind that she may able to change Clinton with her love, but her hope didn't last for long.

"A relationship with a fake commitment never grows for long."

She was almost dead when Clinton punched her in stomach. She fell down from the stairs and had a serious injury in her brain. The injury was so intense that she has to be admitted in intensive care unit. Her doctor said she may not be able to talk or walk for the rest of her life. But God has some different plan for her life. Those days her parents were out of town for three days.

When her parents asked about the incidence Clinton said "we met with an accident while coming from a stage performance."

Considering her situation her parents take her to their home. As Clinton was staying alone her parents insisted him to stay with them, initially he was not agreed but after one month he also shifted there. With constant care and love improvement observed in the health of Katrina. She shows some movement in her body. It's a moment of joy for everyone, but Clinton was not happy. He was in a fear that if she will cure completely she may reveal the truth to her family.

"When you are crazy for a spec made up of love and emotions, everything in front of you seem truth." - Katrina

Clinton started showing a fake act of love and care and to an extent he succeeded. He didn't want to stay there for a long time. Anyhow he managed to convince her parents; with Katrina, they shifted to his place. It was the end of her peaceful living when he started playing the cruel game. Even though he was responsible for the condition of Katrina, he started blaming on her and the most common one was "I am not able to enjoy my life because of you, I am living like a watchman."

He started taking money from her parents for the sake of her treatment without her knowledge.

Katrina started improving with time and his degree of abusive language increased too but as per Clinton everything was her fault and nothing to deal with his behavior. In absence of Clinton she used to stay alone without any supervision, she only knows how she has survived. A staff nurse was appointed for her supervision but it was for part time, 1hr in the morning and 1hr in the evening and in the presence of Clinton only.

"Time never gives a hint before it acts; we have to be always prepared for its curse." - Katrina

She has observed the worst day of her life when Clinton didn't came for two days; she was doing everything in the wheel chair itself. She always used to ask herself "how a person could be so cruel?" The scene continues for two years since she regains her talking. With the help of the nurse she communicated to her family. They informed the police and finally he got punishment for his crime. Katrina came back with her family.

Clinton got punishment for his bad deeds but what about Katrina; she was not able to recover from the fear of domestic violence.

She was mentally ill and not satisfied with what she has now. She was always forced to answer the same question, "It has been six months and don't you think you are over reacting?" She was not able to think, what next, who would marry her or for whom she would live. For her "death is easier than to survive," she attempted suicide after six months, but thanks God she is alive today.

★★★

Lateral Equation#1: It has been six months and don't you think you are over reacting?

The fact: The pain of griever may or may not be fixed within a specific time period, and it hurts the griever when such questions were raised. The griever feels like "being a burden for her/his family."

"For me Clinton is like a pilot of Darkness, I thank God that he helps me to get rid of the darkness so soon, I have a long life forward left." – Katrina

Influence of Reality

"A 33 years old U.S Investment banker
attempted suicide."

Being a member of an affluent family in US is a part of good luck. She is a lucky girl not just because she has a luxurious life but for the priceless love of her parents. She is naughty, sometimes misbehaves with her parents, maybe it's an act of childish; but she is not immature. She respects the values of her family when they are outside she behaves in a very polite way.

Sometimes such behavior surprises her parents, but now they are habitual, they feel proud to have a daughter like Sarah Lee.

She has gorgeous parents too; why gorgeous because when her Dad first tells her his love story he used the word "gorgeous" ten times for her Mum and when she listens the same story from her Mum it was countless for his dad. It's not only confined in their words, when Sarah was in kindergarten, she wanted to marry his Dad; it proves he is. Her life with parents not only limited to stories, she spent most of the times with all sorts of games with them.

"My parents never feel hurt as I have not followed their path, but they are happy because I have the ability to choose my own path."-Sarah

Sarah's parents were very ambitious about her; they have already planted dreams for her better future. And the best thing is, Sarah enjoys the conversation between her parents on this hot chapter. Robert, Sarah's dad had a wish that she will be a banker like him but as per her Mum she will make a career as a doctor. But not any of these career options correlate with the thoughts of Sarah and she wanted to be a Journalist.

Neither Robert nor Kati, Sarah's Mum, it was Sarah's wish that got fruitful.

Sarah got admission in Boston University, in journalism with key focus on broadcast journalism. Everything was perfect as per her predetermined goal; the only thing of concern was 'she will have to stay in hostel', far away from her parents. In initial days she was forced to cry sitting at a corner of her room closing all doors and windows. May be, because in the first 15 days she was staying alone; as her roommate joined her little late. Another reason it was for the first time she was staying away from home.

"Apart from ambition
there is something called
LOVE that never
let me sleep until
it is achieved?" -Sarah

As usual she was sitting in the third bench from right nearby the window when she first saw Robin. Her classroom was in the first floor and there was an ATM below her classroom, Robin was going for the ATM when she had an eye contact with him. He drew her attention at first sight, he was handsome and cute that attracted her but the only hurdle was that he was unknown. Even though she was confused, she started searching him but the question that repeatedly coming in her mind was "where to start?"

Finally she got a clue; the badge he was wearing is of management department.

She started searching over social media networks, she searched over 200 profiles in facebook but she didn't get him. After six months during her annual function she found him next to her; both of them were seating in the same row and nominated best scholar of the year from their respective streams. She was surprised for a moment when Robin said "I think I have seen you before." Sarah smiled from inside and said no, the next thirty minutes ended with a formal conversation and she was successful to get some more information about him.

That day she was unable to sleep till late night thinking of him, she was thinking of sending him 'friend-request' over facebook but she didn't want to take the first move. The next morning started with a good news, everything was under her control by then. She got a text notification from facebook and it was for friend request by Robin. She started for college with a fresh mind and not wanted to show any hurry.

She waited for next seven days and finally when her patience broke down, she accepted the request.

After one month their semester exam was over and Sarah went back home. The relationship grew stronger over text, call and facebook. Sarah started talking to herself, whenever she closed her eyes she saw his face, whenever she prayed, she first pray for him; she was in love with him. Her vacations were over and she went back to BU, she reached there in an evening and was eagerly waiting for the next morning. She was very much excited to meet Robin but her dreams were crushed in a moment when she got a call from her Mum.

The next morning, the headlines of all major newspaper was "A 33 year's old U.S Investment banker committed suicide."

The incidence happened at around 11pm of last night. When Sarah was about to sleep, she got a call from her Mum to get back immediately and it was the saddest night of her life.

These are the days of Economic recession in 2008 when Robert Lee had to resign from his job against his consent and when he tried to imagine the adverse effect in his life he didn't able to move further.

In the words of Christina, Sarah's Mum "Robert was not happy with what was going on, in his life, he always said I am not doing anything right for my family, I have no future."

Two days before his suicide he got some calls for clearance of EMI, sometimes threatening. He was a soft hearted person and has never experienced such psychic pressure before. He started considering himself worthless. At the time of grief it's a human tendency that we consider ourselves worthless, depression creates hurdles in the way of being active.

This was the first instance in which Jenifer didn't meet the victim, but the truth was very painful.

What she had concluded was on the basis of the inputs by Christina. Christina and Sarah were now a part of a grief support group and they contribute a major role to boost morale of other grievers, sometimes before they were in need of it. When Jenifer met the therapist of Christina, she got the fact behind Robert's suicide.

When Robert was in depression even though Christina was there to support him, she always tried to boost his morale for a better future rather listening to his present.

***

Lateral Equation #2: You have a capability to rebuild your strength.

The fact: The griever always wants someone who can listen to him/her. The best way to help him/her heal is "say little and do what can be done to help ease burdens"

Robert may be with Sarah today, if Christina has the answer of this equation, she may be able to minimize the influence of reality.

Someone of Nobody

"The darker the night, the brighter the stars, The deeper the grief, the closer is God!" – Fyodor Dostoyevsky

Settled next to a large and beautiful park, the village of Hwen is home to family of Cecilia. The village itself looks dull with its blackened rooftops and rotten fields. Even there are number of reasons to settles at Hwen, Cecilia's parents wanted to shift from Hwen considering Cecilia's higher education. When Cecilia was 14 years old her family shifted to Austin, Texas where she got admission to a residential Girls School.

"I was excited
thinking of the new place,
new environment,
and new friends." -Cecilia

Cecilia was jolly in nature but in her routine work she is a good finisher. This makes her unique; she never left any job in between. Her passion for her goals never let her sleep till she reached the desire goal. Despite grew up in a small village, Cecilia was very intelligent and career conscious. She never had a serious relationship with a guy. Her friends finds something wrong in her but for Cecilia; she was in an intention that her inclination towards her career might be a reason of her lack of interest in boys; the idea of being a lesbian never knocked her mind.

"It was not just an accident a planned incidence at a perfect time and a perfect place scripted by a perfect author (Sazia); Cecilia not aware of."

During a summer vacation, Cecilia along with her friends, were planning for an outing. On that day she met Toni, through her mutual friends. She finds Toni as cute, amicable and sexually magnetic; a girl she was always looking for inside some corner of her subconscious mind; who can fulfill her all desire and be a good companion in long run too. They became good friends with a very short span of time. Cecilia started enjoying the sweetness of life. She finds her living full of fun with Tony, as it was her first serious relationship, a perfect one she always looking for.

She didn't able to recall how things were changing very quickly. A career conscious girl turns in to a fun loving butterfly.

As the relationship is not natural and Cecilia's family values were backed by traditional forces, being perfectness in relationship, things were not so easy for both of them. With times they experienced a lot of things those were going against their ways. Cecilia's parents were not agreed with her broad vision.

Toni belongs to a middle class family living with her Mum; her Mum was 55years of old and no one to look after her, except Toni. Even though her Mum was not happy with the relationship of Cecilia and Toni; she has no other options than accepting the fact. After a repetitive approach by Toni, her Mum has to give the approval. Finally a happy moment for the couple came when Cecilia and Toni settled at Toni's place. It was a new life for Cecilia as she never imagined for an easy approval from Toni's Mum. Cecilia has taken all necessary measures to please her.

"Things were not as charming as what actually portrayed to Cecilia, with times she started aware of the actual scene around her life."

At an age of 65 Toni's Mum passes away fighting with a heart disease. During those days Cecilia was jobless and the relationship of Toni with other girls hurting Cecilia from inside. Toni was so upset with too much interference of Cecilia in her life and for circumstances afterwards she started taking drugs. With times Cecilia realized that she was going towards a direction probably she never wanted to. Cecilia finds a drastic change in the behavior of Toni in a short span of time.

Tony was not physically violent but started abusing her with words. Toni blamed his abusive behavior on stress from work.

It was one of the biggest test of her life that "how Cecilia will manage the relationship?" Cecilia was not happy with the relationship, but she knew no one will take care of Toni if she leaves her. The few sweet words she received as an apology from Toni, with respect to his abusing behavior is just because of Cecelia's add on care towards Toni.

Cecilia was living with some hope inside, the memories of the past, the good times and hoping that things may change with time.

The real life show of Cecilia goes on further, but there was no change in Toni's behavior. They had a joint bank account with credit facilities which was always over credited. Toni always blamed Cecilia despite all major transactions was made by Toni. Every times Cecilia responded to it, Toni replied "mind your own business and ask me only when you will not get food or fuel for your car." Cecilia was living with blindfolds and not even aware of why she is not able to respond the situation and staying with Toni since so long with such a pathetic atmosphere.

With times extended kindness of Cecilia forced Toni to consider the facts around.

Toni was able to understand the pain of Cecilia. After two years without any physical intimacy or affection, Toni suggested Cecilia to move on and start with a fresh relationship. Things became little lighter for Cecilia as the suggestion was from Toni's end. She finally decided to move on.

After few months Cecilia met Sazia at a coffee shop. Both were friends since college days. Sazia was lesbian too but not accepted the truth during college days like Cecilia did. Cecilia was in need of a fresh relationship just Sazia has to ignite the desire, that she mages to.

Sazia: I am observing you since few months, you are spending time alone.

Cecilia: yeah, I left her (Toni) and living separately since three months.

Sazia: Toni was unconscious when I met her last time; I was shocked with her behavior.

Cecilia: She is completely changed now; she started taking drugs and alcohol.

Sazia: Somewhat I was aware of; but I never wanted to come between you and Toni.

Cecilia: I can understand, umm…

Sazia: Initially when I introduced her with you; the way Tony flirt was shameful.

Cecilia: yeah, you tried to give some hint, but I was an idiot.

Sazia: You came back! It's good. Things will be OK soon

On insistence of Sazia, Cecilia shifted to her place. Cecilia finds some ease in her living as today she is with someone with whom she can share her feelings and spent quality time. One Sunday Sazia was not at home so Cecilia decided to go to meet Toni. Even though the relationship is not at its usual depth but Cecilia still have some soft corner in her heart for Toni. It's around 2pm when she reached Toni's place as she walked through the bedroom she founds Toni and Sazia slept together. Cecilia was shocked for an instance and came back to her place.

Even after a long time spending with Sazia; she was not able to see the other face of Sazia what she has observed today. Situation forced her to end up the new relationship.

Cecilia shifted to a new place at Austin. She was so depressed that she confined herself inside the four walls of her room and kept herself apart from outside world. She didn't go out at all from her place initially for the first three months but find some ease with times. She started hating herself. Nobody from her friend circle could understand; what is going through in her life.

She can't show the facts to the outside world as it was her second crisis, and everyone around in a thought that, every time it was her fault she didn't able to hold the relationship.

Toni started writing mails with abusing strokes; in Cecilia's words threats and Cecilia never used to respond those mails. Cecilia was forced to break all communications with Toni; but the memories with him of her near past were very painful. Things were very drastic when she finds images of Toni and Sazia over social sites. She became isolated; she didn't let anyone get close to her. Her behavior in past with her parents didn't let her go back to them.

After losing a big span of her valuable life she finally wanted to recover from the grief. She began to read about self help books.

She contacted some domestic violence recovery community, where she got exposure to experiences of similar cases followed by counseling. Additionally she has gone through self help courses. In a short span of time she began to acknowledge the reality of what was happening with her life. Her transformation from a stage once where she wanted to kill herself to this stage is just because she changed her thoughts. Earlier she was like "Everything was the will of God," but now for her "our thoughts are the pilots of grief."

Once she worked on constructing her thoughts she finds a change in her life.

★★★

Lateral Equation#3: "Everything was the will of God."

The fact: "God helps those who help themselves."

I was feeling like "someone of nobody," but today after practicing the fact of these lateral equations "my heart says I am the perfect one." -Cecelia

Dead at the Dark

"So it's true, when all is said and done,
grief is the price we pay for love."
– E.A. Bucchianeri

Looks snug and comfortable; it has been build with sandstone and has white pine wooden decorations. Small, triangular windows let in plenty of light and have been added to the house in a mostly asymmetric way. The roof is low, triangular and layered and is covered with grey wood shingles. Despite all the luxury kissing his feet he is searching for peace around these four walls. This home is of Smith; a tall and handsome guy with a kind approach toward this cruel world.

Those days, he was unhappy with the circumstances he was evidenced in the near past. He was depressed for losing his best buddy of his life, Sooky.

When Smith was 15 years of old Sooky came to his life. With the soft touch of Sooky in his life Smith found a lot of joys and it helped him not to be so bored anymore. With the companion of Sooky, Smith got more engaged in fun rather than books and puzzles. In the initial days he used to teach her going for bathroom outside and on papers. She used to punish Smith for his laziness. To wake up early Smith never asked for a Nescafe, but it was an effect of Sooky's call always.

"Smith's grandma always says, those who laugh more get hurt more. Was she going to evidence it in Smith's life?"

When she grew up, she started following Smith for morning walk and Smith enjoyed her companion too. If she teamed off Smith just be shouting "Shhh… shhh..." and she was coming back. As Sooky needed some exercise everyday Smith did it too and being a part of it, he got benefited. Sometimes his family members were becoming a part of the show. The funniest moments when his grandma joined them and she got some exercise too, may be due to Smith's childish desire. In winter they took different root for morning walk and Smith tracked cock, when Smith would lose the tracks, it's Sooky who would find them.

Sooky's cuteness attracted Smith in such a way that he wanted to have her in every moments of his life. He always wanted her companion, even while going for school. Inside the school he always wished how early the bell would ring and he could meet her.

Even though Smith was not aware of the actual birth day of Sooky, his entire family has been celebrating the birthday of Sooky every year on the day when she first came to his home for the first time. Like every member of his family, it always the luckiest day for Sooky as she got little extra hug from all his family members along with delicious foods. Smith always carried a picture of him with Sooky in his wallet and updated every year on her birthday.

Smith didn't know how early he grown up with tons of best memories with Sooky. Now he became an Architect working in an MNC infrastructure wing at Los Angeles. One day Smith was searching some important documents while going for a meeting. Smith was little bit in a hurry as he wanted to reach the meeting location before time. Sooky was not there, and he wanted to go outside without her knowledge. Smith got his documents, put his coat and started for the meeting. When Smith asked his driver for Car, he felt something pulling his trouser and it was Sooky; it might be usual for Sooky as she was not aware of the priority. But Smith lost his temper and slapped her.

Sooky was aware that Smith was doing something wrong she pulled him back to home, where Smith's grandma was waiting for.

Grandma: Today is the last day of filing Tax and you are missing some papers here.

Smith: Oh Sooky, I am sorry (Sooky wagged her tail.)

Smith thanked his grandma too.

Grandma: Smith, offer her a piece of meat.

Smith: Darling I am getting late please do this favor for me.

"I came home little late
that night
and found Sooky dead."
-Smith

Sooky was not just a dog; she was a part of his life. Sooky passed away at an age of mere thirteen. Smith and she had spent thirteen good years together. Before her death, those days were quite harder for Sooky as she was sick and declining her health, she stopped eating properly. Few days back, Sooky and Smith's grandma went for a health test of Sooky which revealed that her kidney was starting to fail. But it's shocking for Smith that it's so soon. Sooky was with Smith's grandma when she passed away and sometimes Smith feels guilty of not being there.

"Smith buried her in the backyard and sometimes she came in his dreams; seemed young and full of energy to remind Smith that she is okay wherever she is."

It's natural to be a victim of sadness, grief and intense pain when a pet dies; specially someone like Sooky who was a part of Smith's life. He was not only grieving for a pet but for a guide, a companion, the best buddy. Loss of pet is a personal experience followed by grief it's very unpractical to let people make understand how you feel.

For Smith he experienced the grief in waves with high and low intensity in different span of time.

Initially it was very difficult for Smith to make his family understand what was going on in his mind, but his actions were reflecting his grief. Everyone was in a thought that things will be alright once he will be habitual with Sooky's absence, but something was hindering his happiness. Even after few years from the death of Sooky; a sight, a sound, or a special occasion with her memory has the potential to push him towards grief. When it continues for a long time he finally opts for a treatment.

★★★

Lateral Equation#4: "It was just a dog."

The fact: "Sometime pets become a part of your life and his loss can make us insane."

"I lost him at dark, and his loss made my life dark. Pets have the equal importance in our life like human beings if someone really loves them." -Smith

Result of Joy

"One day, in retrospect, the years of struggle will strike you as the most beautiful." – Sigmund Freud

Tiara is the only daughter of her parents residing at Oceanside, California. Tiara started showing interest on her profession since childhood, at an age of twelve she started doing hair at home. She was nineteen when she was at college but started working with her cousin's shop part time. Tiara, a 5.6" girl having beautiful build proved to be a style icon for her friends. She used to hit gym thrice a week and take special care on her food habits. There's something extraordinary about Tiara, perhaps it's her attitude or simply her perseverance that people love to be in her circle.

After college she moved out to Tucson and started her career as a cosmetologist; a hard core profession that requires both physical and emotional exhaust. She was maintaining the diet plan there too. She loved her profession and because of her amicable nature she was able to maintain a good client relationship. As a professional, she proved herself as most trusted people among her client's. Everything was on its way and she was enjoying her profession too. She got success and fame at his new work destination, what she left at Oceanside was only the love of her family.

"Sometimes our highest goal becomes our big enemy when we move towards our goal blindly without focusing on the path we follow."

She was excessively engaged in her profession and not getting time for cooked food and no one was there with her to take care of. She experienced a change in her life style and there after she never thought of workout again and started spending most of the time in party and fun. During this transition she ignored her life style, and she gained 20kg in a period of ten years.

She was facing the adverse effect of obesity since last five years, but her party mood never cared for it.

Her boyfriend left her five years back as she was excessive fat. In spite of all such ups and downs she never looked back. Now she turns thirty; she started experiencing more adverse effects of obesity. Being overweight puts extra pressure on joints and limbs making activities quite difficult and sometimes painful; what Tiara is experiencing now. She reported asthma too. She consulted with her doctor. He suggested that if she will not change her life style it may push her towards death. During those days her cupboards were full of pills.

"Once I was so depressed that I wanted to kill myself with excessive intake of sleeping pills, thanks to God today I am alive." -Tiara

Being a cosmetologist she has learnt only one success mantra "before" and "after"; what she always says to her clients; today it was her turn. It is human nature as most of the time we are worried thinking "what people will think about us" and she was the victim this time. She started to realize her eating disorder and ashamed of her body. It even hurts more when someone specifically her clients started pointing her physic. She was embarrassed to join a gym because of her heavyweight. She started running but couldn't maintain the rhythm for more than two minutes.

As insisted by one of her client, she joins a meditation class and it helps her to kill some negativity of her life.

After lots of efforts she managed to avoid fast food and managed to arrange cooked meals. Obesity is an output of calories intake versus calories exhausted. She started counting her average calories intake per day, and it was 900 to 1000 only. She wonders that she was not taking adequate calories, but thatwas not working. She was so depressed with her progress graph. After some unease nights without having sound sleep she decided to go for a small walk after dinner every night. And she was able to continue the rhythm for the month; she managed to lose 2kg weight with this little effort.

"The problem is not with her weight, but with her thoughts that pulling her back before initiating any action."

She was quite happy with this small output and it inspired her to move further. She subscribed to health magazines and watched media channels. As per those instructions she started working out; in the initial days it was like living in hell as an outcome of it she couldn't able to walk or drive car for two days but she didn't give up and her efforts. It started giving results, within next six months she lost additional six KGs. She found a boost in her self esteem and her asthma too went away. She finally joined a gym and kept going as per pre-defined goal sets.

The whole journey of last two years in her life was a big lesson of her life.

She found a big change in her life. Everyone around her started admiring her. Finally she started being happy; giving up KFC for a period of two years didn't cost her much. Again she became the center of attraction in her group. It's nothing but a feeling of awesomeness when everyone wants to hang out with you. Her ex wanted to come back again but Tiara didn't want to look back again.

"Our life gives us a number of clues in the way of life lessons, to know who is right and who is wrong."

It's really a nice feeling receiving complements, but people sometimes didn't able to convey the actual meaning what they pretend to. She started receiving texts, asking the secrets of her health. On a summer evening while she was moving for swimming pool her cook said, Madam you are looking different, you must be trying to catch some gold fish.

Like every positive output has some negative impacts, she started receiving complaints backed by jealousy. Sometimes like you are too skinny, boys like girls with curve, you will not able to enjoy your life anymore.

After certain span of time her friends started ignoring her, because of her, self centered attitude specifically towards eating habits. The other side of jealousy is that it encourages rumors and it's not always possible to clarify your inside story. This is the right time to know who your true companions are. What she has learned from her experience "people sometimes are with you to make laugh of you" and those who really care for you always follow you.

★★★

Lateral Equation#5: People commit suicide because of grief.

The fact: It's not grief but negative thoughts, can kill you. A positive thought has the power to dominate thousands of negative psychological blocks.

What I was and what I am today is a result of joy for "what I wanted to be." -Tiara

The Secret's Truth

"For Mercy it's not the thought but the act that displays the depth of love."

Its immaturity or achildish act he didn't know, but those days his ego was adding spices to his attitude. He was feeling like having a life with absence of love and care from his parents. His attitude was saying from inside "nobody is there to understand my feelings, I am not getting enough freedom, I don't know, what is the problem with this cruel world and the surrounding people. How can people behave like the worst way with a small little kid?"

It's not the only case of Mercy but most of the kids surrounding him have similar complaints; as appeared to Mercy.

For Mercy the acts of his parents were not justified; he wanted to fight against their cruel will. Whether time changes our thoughts or thought changes with time it's debatable. But today he is matured and has developed a potential to judge things or acts to determine what is right and what is wrong. His thought process changed with time and life events or experiences. Now he understands the theory of thought and act, now he respects the acts of his parents and he is following their path, "love is not with the acts but with the thoughts." Today he became an ideal father of two little cute children aged ten and four. Today he can understand how caring his parents were and how perfect the scene of staying with his parents was! He understands the purpose behind his parents' act and is now treating his own kids in the same way.

"The portrait of his past was partially erased by God and he is searching for those erased portions."

Mercy was graduated from Anderson School of Management, University of California. Few weeks before his final exam of MBA, Mercy got a call from his uncle at around 3 AM and he asked him to came back home immediately. He tried to ask him the reason but his uncle somehow manages to hide the fact. He took the next flight for Boston at 4 AM; he assumed that something was wrong but not getting any hints.

When he reached there, his sister Maria, told him to reach Beth Israel Deaconess Medical Center and there he was informed that his parents were in ICU.

Mercy asked the doctor to meet his parents, but they didn't agree as operation was going on after few moments he was allowed to visit his parents for a short time. His father's face was not identifiable due to the accident. Mercy listened to the last words of his father he said "your mom is no more" and he too passed away. Mercy was chasing an unknown goal that can't be achieved, trying to hide the saddest truth. It hurts more when we know from inside that we are not going to achieve anything, but we can't live without that mundane desire. He was twenty three years old when his parents left him alone.

"Mercy felt like he was lost in an ocean where Tsunami was dancing with him, waves of different emotions were playing with his mind and he was not getting any way to go out of it, he was paralyzed with his thoughts."

It was not for the first time for Mercy that grief has kissed his feet. Life is playing with his emotions since he was a little kid. When he was in class 5th he was staying with his uncle's place. During a vacation when he was coming back home with his uncle, they met with an accident and his uncle died on the spot. Nobody was there at the place where it happened. He was crying continuously for hours but no one to help.

After three hours an old man came to help him; he called the ambulance and the scene after words were very pathetic for his psyche.

When Mercy look back to his past and recall those moments it still hurt him.

Those days his parents were with him to guide him; in the darkest path of sorrow and grief of loss. But this time his moments of sadness were quite different; nobody was with him to hold his hands, to guide his way in this moment of sadness. Being addressed by the cruel act of misfortune before he is prepared; this time he was acting in a quite different way. He was not appeared to be sad all the time as people expected him to be.

He rarely cried, trying to act like normal but the effect of the grief was so deeper that he was not able to concentrate on his acts.

A schedule was a must for him to recall all the time that "he is not weak," to remind him he has a determined life goal for his living. He was forcing himself to wake up early in the morning; trying to act as per a predetermined schedule. Mercy was trying to project a happy mood, with a good appearance to the outside world. For his surroundings it was good to see that, he was coping with the grief very well. But it's not so easy to carry the plastic smile always. He proved himself an outstanding actor for the outer world but things were different from inside. Things he used to love were now assignments for him and he was forced to work on them. He was forced to take food against his interest, to please his dear ones.

Unfortunately in internet most of the recommendations of psychological counselors were not tagged with "as directed by your therapist."

Mercy started being isolated inside the room in most of the time. He was aware that he will not be able to face the outer world with a fake smile holding all his pain inside. He wanted to get some help but not able to share his feelings with anyone asstays alone at home. Most of the times he engaged himself in surfing internet to get some help for his grief. He got some reference over there and planned to implement it on himself.

"I developed a belief that being engaged in more activities may help me to ignore the grief." -Mercy

During the time of grief it is not expected from the griever that he can differentiate "what is wrong and what is right." Mercy was not aware of right application of the term "engage in more activities." He started being involved in certain task in most of his time. The only time left with him was at night, during that time too, he was not able to ignore the memories of his past.

As an outcome of excessive engaging works he has to suffer from loss of health and eye strain.

After a couple of months it was his father's birthday came, such life events are a reminder of strong emotional bonding; the accumulated strengths of Mercy burst suddenly. A continuous flow of emotional waves started crushing him to a place where he was not getting a way to escape. A time has knocked in his life when he experienced the darkest point of grief and sadness; some echo's inside telling his self, 'you are gone made'.

He stopped caring "what is going around him, what people thinking about him, just like a mute climax of his life," he started crying louder.

Finally he wished that, "the people who care for him should know the fact," and he didn't want to live a fake life to make people happy. He was so depressed and wanted help to move out from the ocean of grief. Mercy didn't able to sit for the final exam, upon consultation by his teacher he revealed everything, what was going on in his life. The teacher referred Mercy to a counselor. He started therapy afterwards after couple of months he experienced some good feelings for life.

With continuous effort he is able to reach a position today where he can talk about his loss, without a lie or a fake smile.

★★★

Lateral Equation#6: You need to be more active.

The fact: It's not beneficial for the bereaved to indulge in neither excessive activities nor being isolated.

"In grief people often blindly follow what the elders or friends guide, but not in the right way. So it's very essential to understand the secret truth of those lateral equations which come to our mind while we are in grief." - Mercy

Punished by the Nature

"Some old wounds never truly heal and bleed again at the slightest word." – George R.R. Martin

Caring and doting nature with a frame of simplicity makes her unique. With these adjectives it was obvious for her to pull herself into the center of attraction in her social sphere. Everything in her life was on the desired track she always wished for. Initially when things were not parallel with her preferred career option, she started her career from a reality show; but now she is into modeling, her desired career option. During those days she was quite engaged in a short commercial advertisement; for one of a leading hair oil brand of US where she met Oscar for the first time.

In a short span of time the friendship between them reached to a higher level. Emily got married at an age of twenty with Oscar; a smart and dynamic person having an affluent industrial family background.

In the initial years of her marriage, she didn't want to have any kid, may be for the first five years; till the time she will be twenty five years of age. She didn't want to have any add on responsibility in between these partying moments. She was on birth control, for a period of five years and kept a focus on her career and enjoyment.

Oscar wanted to engage in some career option different from his league.

Belonging to an industrial family, he didn't want to join his family business. He was working for an MNC, leading its corporate office at New York. The fun mood of newly married couple exceeded some good years, afterwards both of them started paying more attention into their respective profession rather than their personal life.

Everything was perfect for the outside world; as reflecting from a glossy mirror. After a certain span of time Oscar felt the absence of a baby in their life. On the insistence of Oscar, Emily agreed upon it. As per Emily's wish time was playing its game, she reached to an age of twenty five by that time and Emily too wanted to plan for kid after twenty five.

Emily stopped taking pregnancy pills and stated taking all necessary measure to conceive.

For every woman it's a most precious desire to get pregnant and for Emily's too. She started whispering while in sleep and used to play with cute babies in dreams. Her subconscious mind was playing with her thoughts. She was very curious for her new dream, she started building thoughts of a new future, she was trying to get pregnant; she started taking care on every possible act to get pregnant, like timing of intercourse, food pattern, diagnostic procedures and all such stuff every woman does for such priceless dreams.

"Emotions of trying to conceive are more challenging than treatment of infertility." -Emily

They were trying to conceive, never expecting any problems, but after trying for over two years nothing had happened. Emily has started experiencing unusual pains during her periods. They consulted with her gynecologist, she told her it was quite normal to have terrible periods and maybe she was just over reacting. She further suggested her if things will continue to be unusual Emily can visit after three months and not to worry as everything was normal then.

Emily never experienced good time afterwards; her periods became worse, and she was experiencing a very critical life situation both mentally and physically.

After couple of months when she experienced very serious pain they went to her gynecologist, after the normal treatment she got some relief, further Oscar requested for referring Emily's case to a reproductive endocrinologist. They have gone through all possible treatment but nothing worked. Those days Emily was too depressed as she has taken all feasible measure to conceive.

Once Emily was at office meeting hall along with her colleagues for quarterly review, she was diverted towards the window "where a beggar seating with her two kids playing with them," Emily stared counting thoughts of the sacred joy of having kids. Usual discussions were going on between her colleagues before the meeting, one of her colleague initiated discussing about her last anniversary celebrations "celebrating at a hill station leaving their kids at home with their parents." On a lighter note she said "Emily was quite lucky that she has not planned yet for a baby." She further added "I know how nervous I was that day leaving kids at home." Emily smiled for a moment and said yeah you are right dear. That night was one of the saddest nights for her; she cried for about two hours that night.

"Journey becomes difficult when we know the destination but not aware of the right path, may be the supreme power testing your moral and physical stamina."

Lack of information on dealing with grief and getting no direction of help leads to more depression; what Emily was facing those days. Residing in a surrounding of small set up; in a small town she didn't find access to any support group or a qualified counselor to deal with her grief. Oscar's parents suggested them for adopting a baby and they agreed upon it. During such a painful era of Emily's life Serena came to her life as a ray of hope; their adoption went through.

"Was this the end of her pain or she was searching something that can't be chased?"

Emily experienced some echoes of peace and serenity as an outcome of the soft knock of Serena's sweetness in her life. Serena's presence has proved to fill some emptiness in her life, but up to what extent was still a question mark for her family. Oscar was aware of the same and was taking all possible steps to motivate Emily.

For Emily the new chapter of her life was quite peaceful and added some happiness in her life but not able to diminish all her pains completely; as she was confused between the facts behind her grief "it was for missing a baby or just her infertility."

If "missing a baby," it must be ended with Serena's presence, but she didn't feel so. As in some sort of life situations; a social occasion, a memory or a dream were trying to kiss her "with the long term grief of infertility" or "not having her own baby" she was not able to respond those situations properly.

"Not being able to have her own baby; a tag that never let her live happily, demoralizing her inner self."

Emily was of the opinion that "by avoiding discussion of her grief, she may manage to discard it from her mind." But the fact was "not discussing about her grief, she was allowing the grief to play with her psyche." As an outcome of it she used to become thought paralyzed; its outcome started creating an impact on her actions and worked heavily, most of the time she used to stand idle or appeared playing with the thoughts inside her mind.

Nobody in her family was happy with her acts. It was very difficult for others too, to understand the fact as she was trying to hide the truth.

An unusual change in her behavior within a small span of time forced Oscar to think on it. After frequent consultation she revealed the fact behind the scene. Situation demanded to search for a support group or a good counselor; to get rid of her grief. She started searching over the internet but she did not find a suitable group that can help her; still she was not able to justify her mind that these groups will do the miracle that medical science could not.

With constant motivations by Oscar she consulted with a therapist. It took almost one year for her to get rid of the situation and today she is able to enjoy all her dreams with Serena and her family.

★★★

Lateral Equation#7: The pain will go away faster if you ignore it.

The fact: The bereaved always wants to talk about their loss and each time a griever talks about the loss, a layer of pain is shed.

"Earlier I was feeling like I am a victim of the Nature, but once I understand the equations of insanity, my life has changed."-Emily

The Shadow Vanishes

A man in his dream asked God
"Please drop me to that planet of my
dreams, where I first met her, I can
survive without food and shelter, not
without her."
And God replied
"I can't help you, I can only guide you,
and you have to help yourself."

Silver, long laired hair tight in a bun reveals a round, time-worn face. Piercing pink eyes set narrowly within their sockets. Several moles are spread gracefully on her right cheek and leave an amusing memory of her fortunate adventures. Clara Ashlin, a true romanticist among her race. There's something seductive about her, perhaps it's her persistence or perhaps it's simply her warmth. But nonetheless, people tend to be curious about her. Clara was the perfect girl, Marlon always dreamt of.

Clara and Marlon were childhood friends and were not in contact since ages.

Marlon had a restaurant at Crescent City, California. He was looking for someone who can adjust with his grandma and in times can manage the restaurant. When Clara broke up with her guy she tried to initiate contact with Marlon. With a short span of time both got closer with each other. On insistence of Clara, Marlon offered her to join his restaurant. It was a sweet experience for Marlon to accompany with Clara at his restaurant.

Everything was awesome with the pair with a new trend in life. Both of them started experiencing a new tone with party, drinks and lots of fun.

Marlon's parents were separated when he was ten years old and he was staying with his father. Two years back his father died in an accident. Since then Brionna, Marlon's grandma was staying with Marlon. She was 73 years old; her old age was demanding Marlon to marry at the earliest, so that her wife may take care of her. But he was not able to convey his inner feelings to Clara. Finally Brionna asked Marlon to propose Clara for marriage. So Marlon had to initiate the knot now, upon the requirement of her grandma. In the next morning while going for the restaurant Marlon started the discussion:

Marlon: Clara, for some reason, I'm attracted to you.

Clara: smiled and said "Prove it dude!"

Marlon: Sweetheart, what did you bury in the garden I don't know but it is spreading fragrance of love?

Clara: Are you kidding? I think you're not 'fine!' Tell directly what you want to say?

Marlon: sometimes action says louder than words.

Marlon kissed her lips tightly and said we are going to bind with an engagement knot. From next month onwards you will not be my girlfriend and you will be......

After one month they got married, and all emotions were now official for both of them. Clara shifted to Marlon's place. Brionna welcomed her with extended sweetness and love. With passing times Clara proved herself a loving daughter in law to Brionna. Within a period of two years, love made their family little bigger, they were blessed with a baby girl, Kiara; a very cute and goody-goody baby girl. Birth of Kiara added a new fragrant to their love life.

After few years of Kiara's birth, Clara developed a sense of inferiority with Brionna. Marlon's friends were now enemy for Clara as they were more inclined towards Brionna. With passing times the inferiority became jealousness; because Marlon was giving much respect to her grandma, may be due to her old age or traditional values. Clara wasbecoming upset with the life style of Marlon.

She was searching for opportunities to belittle Marlon and for Marlon this was the time to make a habit of addressing some common ones like, "baby your clothes were silly," "your hobbies were full of stupidity," "you are not good at sex," "you are not humorous".

Now her inferiority turned into temper. In temper sometimes she tried to hit him physically. She forced Marlon to have sex most of the times; to let him prove a good husband. Situation became worst when Clara kept herself away from all household works and made her busy in late night partying and drinking. Somehow it was affecting the life of Kiara, Marlon had a slight hint of it, but Marlon was kind and could not leave Clara knowing she has no one in her life other than Marlon, Kiara and his grandma.

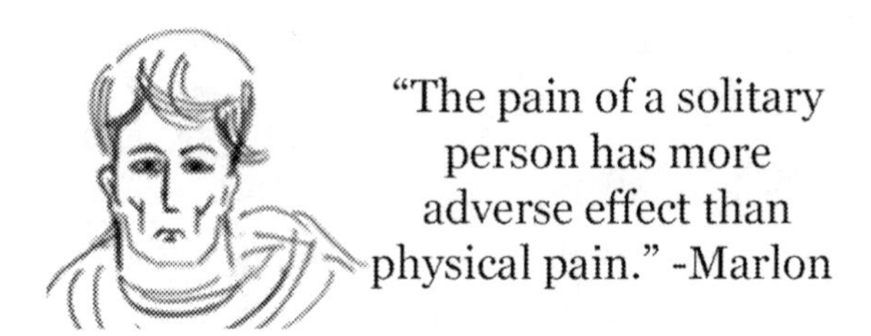

Marlon tried to convey Brionna about the behavior of Clara but Brionna always finds fault in Marlon. She always wished for "how things will fix with ease" but nothing worked. After few years Brionna passed away and there was no one between Marlon and Clara to fix the relationship issues. Marlon started responding to the assault of Clara and it was beyond the acceptance level of Clara's ego. A day has come when her ego didn't allow her to continue with the relationship. She decided to leave Marlon; she took away Kiara with her. She never thought for a second "what will be the impact of her haphazard lifestyle to Kiara."

On the other side, with the loss of his love and his baby, life became difficult for Marlon. For the outside world, it was the fault of Marlon that he didn't manage to hold the relationship. In such a scenario it was not feasible for Marlon to share his pain to anyone, he was forced to live with the pains holding inside. He was depressed with saddest feelings of solitary. His loneliness started killing him like the outburst of slow poison and he was not getting any sense of direction further to live, to move on. Solitude hurts even more; because we don't have anyone to share with.

"When stupidity reaches its highest level, we act rubbish knowingly."

When love turns into poison it hurts more, and knowingly we take interest in consuming that poison, what Marlon was doing then. Even though he was aware that, both are diverted towards different paths, he was waiting for her which was not viable at that moment, without the will of Clara. For Marlon she is like oxygen for his life and he can't imagine life without her.

Marlon tried to cross all hurdles to adopt the silliest stuff for fixing the relationship, he worked on every suggestion his friends suggested, to get her back. In reality he was trying to transform himself to be the person he never wanted to be. But finally time changed, and he realized that he can't change the feelings of others by imitating an imaginary self. He further realized that he is just harming himself by doing all these stuffs.

During this transition of knowing the ugly truth, he harmed himself a lot. He didn't want to proceed further in the darker path. He wanted to get rid of his grief. He consulted with a therapist. Marlon shared all her painful episodes with the therapist.

Marlon: A man always needs his wife and daughter.

Therapist: You stand there and accuse her, but you need to think on "where you put yourself this time? Is it going to heal your grief?"

Marlon: I am all solitary and not able to view any direction to move forward.

Therapist: Being solitary is a part of our life. To stop feeling solitary you need to portray the thoughts (including sadness, anger, and frustration) of your solitary in to actions. As you will start to share your thoughts, you will be more able to begin new changes in your life.

As the ego inside did not let Marlon share his feelings to his friends, his therapist was the only person he could share his thoughts. He shared everything to him. Therapist further said, "Sought out real friends from your profession and initiate your own assessment of a positive life. I have seen a number of similar instances where most of the people came back to their life they wanted to be after a very painful era of their life that even can't be imagined."

"I can't help you, I can only guide you, and you are the one who can help yourself."

Marlon was under the shadow of a blind belief that "grieving alone will heal everything," but it doesn't. He came back to his normal life once he removed the blindfolds he was carrying over his eyes.

★★★

Lateral Equation#8: "grieving alone will heal everything."

The fact: "It's not grieving alone, but sharing your grief and acting upon your weakness can heal the grief."

"I was living in shadow, and my life has changed once the shadow vanished." - Marlon

Hatred of Time

"Scars have the strange power
to remind us that our past is
real." –Cormac McCarthy

Red, short hair was slightly covering a thin, sad face. Heavy hazel eyes, set buried within their sockets, watched faithfully over the window. They've worshipped for so long. Freckles were spread elegantly around her nose and cheekbones and left an amusing memory of her reckless luck.

Emma Kinton stood towering; even God was testing her capability to face immense pressure of Grief. There was something charming about her, perhaps it's her odd friends or perhaps it was simply her clumsiness, people wanted to be within her circle. Jenifer was one amongst them. Emma and Jenifer were childhood friends. Due to the doting nature of Emma, Jenifer was fond of her. Jenifer used to share all her secrets to Emma since childhood, but due to some unavoidable circumstances, they have not met since long.

Shibi was the only person of her life who cared for her. Jenifer has been to Shibi's place for some personal help, where she met Emma. It was an immense pleasure meeting someone she always wanted to, Jenifer thought of sharing her story. This time something unusual happened, it was Emma's turn. Jenifer's excitement didn't last long when Emma revealed something unexpected; a darken chapter of her life. Jenifer was shocked for a moment knowing what was going on in Emma's life. It was not the jolliest friend of her life, the saddest mirror.

Jenifer asked herself "was it scripted by God or I am playing with my life."

Emma was a kind of women who always lived in her dreams. Emma always dreamt of "an old fashioned house should have been built with yellow pine wood having walnut wood decorations. Further large, triangular windows should brighten up the house and have been added to the house in a very symmetric way. The building should be in shape like a circle. The house should be partially surrounded by a covered patio on two sides. The roof should be low, triangular and covered with red wood shingles. One large chimney should sit at the side of the house. The house itself should be surrounded by a gorgeous garden, including hanging grape vines, a pagoda, a pond and many flowers." And today her dream home is in place; a sweet home where Emma recently shifted.

"Without the cuteness of her soft skins, nothing can fill the emptiness of Emma."

Another good news was that "she was pregnant" and waiting for adding some sweetness in her life. She started enjoying all the prettiest moments of her life; doing all silly stuff all pregnant women do. She always wished for a baby girl and started thinking of names for the new member. She was little devotional and always prayed to God that things must go well. And finally the day came in her life when she gave birth to a cute little baby girl; as she always wished for. But the sweet tone of the new member didn't last long.

Her baby had to be diagnosed for some cardiac issue. At one week old; the baby had to spend four days in hospital recovering from the surgery, but nothing worked.

"Tear is a part of my life, even after 9 years things were as it was, with painful moments mixed of emotional thoughts and beliefs. When I talk to others who has suffered from some major loss in their life it works as a relief to my heart, every time I listen, I accumulate some inspiration out of it. But it never lasts for long. I still face days when I cry the whole day." -Emma

Jenifer: "till when you will wait for some good time or some magic by God, you need to act on your grief?"

Emma: "The first year of suffering was the hardest; it was like my baby was always near me, crying for milk and my love. I was kept saying in dreams she was learning to say Mum."

Jenifer: "Stop writing script of your life with your painful thoughts, let God do his duties. It's not the will of God, you are killing yourself. Grief never crush, it creates us. It helps us to find our strengths."

Emma: "Time heals all wounds and I think mine too."

Jenifer: "Time heals all wounds; every one of us heard about it and said it for someone even I also used to say so. But my experience, revealed some different facts to my life."

Jenifer shared her story to Emma to let her know it's not time that heals grief. Jenifer explained why it's not time.

As per dictionary meaning "Heal" refer to "restore to soundness". When we met with an accident or suffer from some disease we are diagnosed and with passing times, it heals too. Most of us have experienced such major or minor incidents in our life, but for such diseases or accidents, pain never lasts for long, it lasts till the period of diagnosis or for a specific period of life same as the healing period. Jenifer further asked "Does time really heal your grief? Does it cure and take away all your pains? Ask your soul, Emma."

Jenifer reminds a verse of the Bible.

Luke 12:22-31 Then He said to His disciples, "Therefore I say to you, do not worry about your life, what you will eat; nor about the body, what you will put on. Life is more than food, and the body is more than clothing. Consider the ravens, for they neither sow nor reap, which have neither storehouse nor barn; and God feeds them. Of how much more value are you than the birds? And which of you by worrying can add one cubit to his stature? If you then are not able to do the least, why are you anxious for the rest?

Consider the lilies, how they grow: they neither toil nor spin; and yet I say to you, even Solomon in all his glory was not arrayed like one of these. If then God so clothes the grass, which today is in the field and tomorrow is thrown into the oven, how much more will He clothe you, O you of little faith?

And do not seek what you should eat or what you should drink, nor have an anxious mind. For all these things the nations of the world seek after, and your Father knows that you need these things. But seek the kingdom of God, and all these things shall be added to you."

"It will be better to spent our energy on reality; the tangible facts, not thoughts of the past."

Time hasn't made people feel better on the death or some major loss; it just dilutes the thought process by creating an emotional distance from the death or loss. Those diluted emotions or thoughts don't hurt as much as they used to. Is it healing? I suppose it's not. It is common in all those people who have experienced the pain of loss or have suffered from some major domestic violence and its impact, but with some reminders of your loss may be followed by some occasion or discussion, the same old pain bubbles up. People who have lost someone in their life 10, 15, 20 or even 50 years still they became upset when they were reminded of it.

Jenifer: If time does anything it's only dilute your feelings; as you are experiencing today.

Emma: So what shall I do?

Jenifer: A complete healing is something when there isn't pain for you for the loss and you will able to share about it whenever you feel. It's all about what you do with the time and the actions you take.

Most of the people waste their valuable time with just thinking of their loss, they never act. What Jenifer did throughout her life and Emma doing now? In everyone's life a time has come when the emotion or loss of pain diluted. But by that time everything was out of track; for a single loss we destroy everything.

"What heals Emma's wound."

She set an appointment for counseling with a grief therapist. She started acting on her thoughts. She started writing her happy moments of her past, to remind her best reasons why she is alive and what goals need to be accomplished. She made an album and collects top 30 photos of her memories when she was most excited, most enjoyed.

When she feels like upset; she travels in her dream worlds with positive thoughts she has collected from past by looking into the album.

Before it was like "everything was written by God and we have no control on our life." She was not physically there in the act of her life. She was thinking she will reach peace soon, time will heal everything. But today she has a vision for her life. She painted all positive goals of her life everywhere inside her bedroom.

And the thing,which is the most rewarding, is "she is the driver of her life story."

Her message to others, "Who was the killer of your dreams? It's you, who abuse yourself, just thinking about your past? You can only help yourself not anyone else. So don't depend on time. Work on your thoughts today. Let's God takes the responsibility of the world and you drive your life journey."

★★★

Lateral Equation #9: "Time will heal everything."

The Fact: "Time is not the healer, but it's the pilot of grief, only action in time can heal your grief."

Turning Point

"The greatest pleasure of this
Universe isto help a person, who is in
grief."–Jenifer

When I asked Jenifer to tell her story, she was not aware that she mayregenerate her strength to do so but today she is in front of you, to break her silence. Her journey from fear to grief and grief to victory, it may help many people those who are in the saddest era of their life journey. Think of those who have lost their family members or a victim of rape, domestic violence or living in aftermath of a disaster.

Every country has a law to punish the criminals for an act of cruelty, but what about those who are the victims; no nation has a statutory framework to monitor the mental illness or grief of those victims. Nothing can compensate their mental stability prior to those unfortunate moments.

When Jenifer tried to find out the reason she wanted to commit suicide, she was shocked for a moment. She didn't want to kill herself because she was in pain, but she was not able to resolve the equations of insanity in her brain. When she met with people like her she experienced the truth; what she is sharing with you all.

What she has achieved till today?

She was "living a life like a Unicorn in a Zoo," "a victim of sexual abuse," "cheated by her Ex-boyfriend," "a victim of domestic violence."

Why she is living in peace?

"She has able to solve the lateral equations of insanity of her mind, now nobody can play with her thoughts, nobody can cheat her emotions."

Some psychiatrist talks that grief followed some stages, like Swiss Psychiatrist Elisabeth Kübler-Ross describes about five stages of grief that is denial, anger, bargaining, depression, and acceptance, popularly known by DABDA.

★Denial: Wherein the griever develops a false sense of hope for reality. For example my ex may get back again, everything will be fine soon.

★Anger: This is the stage wherein the victim needs to blame someone for their loss, like it's a will of God, I hate him or her.

★Bargaining: Simply means negotiation may be like "My Mum will come back if Dad will stop taking alcohol."

★Depression: This involves experiencing sadness when people feel there is nothing else to be done, or things can't be resolved anymore.

★Acceptance: Where the griever begins accept the reality.

Jenifer didn't disagree with these stages but she argues that it's not always the victim goes through these stages, but s/he has to face some lateral equations in his/her psyche whether s/he may be in any stage of grief. When the victim is not able to answer those equations it takes the shape of insanity and s/he can commit suicide at any moment. She has justified it by her personal experience.

"Suicide is when people didn't
able to solve the equations of
insanity." -Jenifer

How to cope up with grief?

To cope up with grief one has to aware of the answers of those lateral equations. As per Jenifer the answers are as below:

- "Time is not the healer, but it's the pilot of grief," only action in time can heal your grief. Most of the people in grief thought that time will heal everything, but without initiating any action they just do kill their reason to be alive. I have seen many people who have lost their near and dear ones 10, 20 or 40 years before and when some life events remind them of their loss they become insane.
- Sometimes it comes to mind "grieving alone" may help in grief, but sharing your grief is a step towards healing.
- God helps those who help themselves. In grief most of us show anger on God, considering "it's a will of God." God is impartial, and he always gives you whatever you wish. If you live in anger you will get similar output. Grief never is an output of the will of God.
- Sometime pets become a part of our life and its loss can make us insane. Words like "it's just a dog or a cat." can hurt the griever. Equal

attention shall be taken for the griever if it's for "a loss of pets or any other loss."

- Questions like "It has been six months and don't you think you are over reacting?" shall be avoided. The pain of griever may or may not be fixed within a specific time period, and it hurts the griever when such questions were raised.
- Griever doesn't prefer to listen to guidance e.g., "You have a capability to rebuild your strength" rather wants someone who can listen to him/her. The best way to help him/her heal is "say little and do what can be done to help ease burdens."
- The pain of griever may or may not be fixed with in a specific period of time and it hurts the griever when questions were raised, "how long?" S/he feels like "s/he is a burden for her/his family."
- It's guided that "The pain will go away faster if you ignore it." But the fact is the bereaved always wants to talk about their loss and "each time a griever talks about the loss, a layer of pain is shed."
- It's not beneficial for the bereaved to indulge in neither excessive activities nor being isolated. So stop forcing to be more active.

- The bereaved always wants to talk about their loss and each time a griever talks about the loss, a layer of pain is shed.
- It's not beneficial for the bereaved to indulge in neither excessive activities nor being isolated.
- It's not grief but negative thoughts, can kill you. A positive thought has the power to dominate thousands of negative psychological blocks.
- The griever always wants someone who can listen to him/her. The best way to help him/her heal is "say little and do what can be done to help ease burdens."

Where she is?

She is living for a noble cause, she has established an NGO named after Kelly to help people those are victims of some social or domestic violence or are in grief.

"What next: Find at least one person who is suffering from grief and let him/her make understand it's not grief that makes us weak, its unsolved lateral equations of insanity."

Let's pray for a happy Universe.

About the Author

Durgesh Satpathy is an Indian author born in Padampur, Odisha, in 1984, and is the second son of Trungalaya and Bhaktaram Satpathy. He has done his Master in Business Administration from KITS, Ramtek. He aims to reform mindsets of people through his writing.